STARTING LINE

© 2011 MATTEL, INC. ALL RIGHTS RESERVED.

978-0-00-742665-2

1 3 5 7 9 10 8 6 4 2

FIRST PUBLISHED IN THE UK BY HARPERCOLLINS CHILDREN'S BOOKS IN 2011

A CIP CATALOGUE RECORD FOR THIS TITLE IS AVAILABLE FROM THE BRITISH LIBRARY.

WWW.HARPERCOLLINS.CO.UK

PRINTED AND BOUND IN CHINA

Vert Wheeler was in his garage, working on his car. He got in and revved the engine.

'These are some hot wheels,' he said to himself. He sped out of his garage and onto the salt flats. But suddenly Sheriff Johnson pulled up alongside him. 'You're speeding,' the Sheriff accused.

'It's not against the law if I'm on the salt flats. And according to my speedometer, I'm doing the speed limit,' Vert replied, swerving off to the right. The Sheriff crashed into an enormous cactus, completely wrecking his car. He screamed furiously after Vert, but Vert was just a cloud of dust on the horizon.

A bizarre-looking sandstorm caught Vert's eye up ahead.

'That's strange. And around here that's as close as it gets to fun!' As he approached the storm, he was buffeted by high winds. He swerved, trying to stay in control, but the winds lifted his car into the funnel cloud. He was pulled into what looked like a portal, then shot out of the other side into a strange landscape he didn't recognise. He skidded to a halt and got out of his car.

'Where in the world, er, the universe, am I?' he wondered. The landscape around him was barren rock.

Then he caught sight of the portal, which was closing rapidly. He leapt towards it, but it disappeared before he could reach it.

Vert heard a female voice calling for help below. He looked over the ledge and saw a strange blue creature being chased by three vehicles. She tripped, dropping a glowing object. Three animal-like creatures got out of the vehicles and began to fight over the glowing object. Another vehicle approached. A wild lion-like creature jumped out and took it from them.

'Give me back the key, Kalus,' the blue creature demanded angrily.

'The battle key belongs to me,' he snarled. The blue creature faced the others defiantly. 'I will not allow you to destroy any more worlds,' she said.

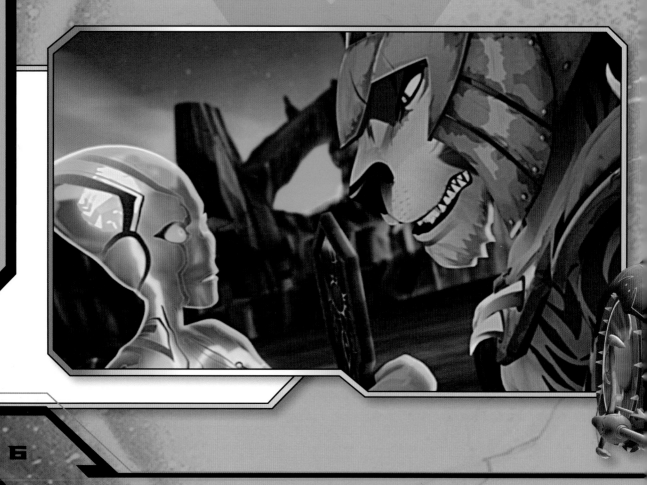

Kalus sneered. 'You are the last of your kind. You can do nothing to stop me!' But he was interrupted by the sound of Vert's car as he leapt off the cliff. Whilst Kalus was distracted, the blue creature grabbed the key and ran for her life. Vert skidded in an arc around her and scooped her into his car before speeding away. Kalus growled in fury and took off after them.

'Who are you? What are those freaky creatures? And where exactly are we?' Vert demanded.

'Those creatures are called Vandals. They are a species of savage conquerors. I am Sage, a Sentient. And we are in an inter-dimensional battle zone. One of many throughout the multiverse.'

Kalus appeared right behind them, and shot a spear on a rope into the rear bumper of Vert's car.

Vert accelerated hard. The tension in the rope caused Kalus's vehicle to flip over, sending Kalus flying.

Sage pressed a button on one of her data strips. An enormous vehicle de-cloaked in front of them and Vert drove inside. The vehicle cloaked again just as the Vandals arrived on the scene.

Inside, Vert looked around in awe. 'What is this thing?'

'A Mobius Command Centre. It functions as a mobile repair station, a storehouse of knowledge, as well as a power source for me,' Sage explained. 'It is damaged beyond repair. Let us hope it has enough energy to perform one last function.' She stepped out of the car and floated up into the air. A platform raised a surprised Vert off the ground. Sage activated a holographic console and took a red chip from inside her chest.

'This is a self-contained power cell that contains blueprints to upgrade your vehicle. This device will analyse you and customise the capabilities of your vehicle to your personality. Unfortunately, all other systems will need to shut down, including the cloaking device,' Sage told Vert.

Outside, the Mobi flickered into view right in front of Kalus. He smiled.

Inside the Mobi, robotic arms added new parts and fresh, sword-like edges to Vert's car. Another robotic arm scanned Vert's body, and a red suit appeared in place of his clothes.

'A high impact, G-force resistant battle suit,' Sage explained. Vert laughed in amazement.

'To complete the bond with your machine, you must name your vehicle,' Sage said.

'The Saber,' he decided. The Saber glowed in sync with Vert's touch as the bond was completed.

Suddenly a siren blared.

'Kalus and his Vandals are near,' Sage said. 'The key will signal to you when you get close to the portal.'

Vert looked alarmed. 'But the portal's gone!'

'This battle key will unlock it,' Sage assured him, attaching the battle key to his car. 'Take the key and lock the portal on the Earth-side. I must travel in hibernation mode to conserve energy.' Sage transformed into a tiny cube, which dropped into Vert's hands.

Vert shot out of the Mobi and headed straight for the Vandals. Kalus snarled. 'Sever, Krocomodo, seize command of the Mobius and strip it of its resources. I will pursue the sub-creature.'

Kalus fired a barrage of arrows, but Vert swerved expertly to avoid them. The Vandal, Hatch, struck out with a scorpion tail from his vehicle, barely missing the Saber.

Inside the Mobi, a self-destruct countdown activated itself. 'It's going to blow!' Krocomodo cried. They shot out of the Mobi seconds before it blew itself to smithereens.

Meanwhile, Vert had spotted a rock formation in the shape of a ramp up ahead. He accelerated towards it and launched himself into the air. Hatch slammed straight into a cliff face, while Vert landed on an upper ledge and sped off. But now Kalus was on his tail. He rammed his chariot into Vert's car. The Saber came dangerously close to the edge of the cliff.

Vert rammed Kalus. Kalus lost control of his chariot. The battle key shot off the bonnet of the Saber, forming a stormshock ahead. Vert rocketed through the portal. He blasted onto the salt flats and jumped out of the Saber. But the portal was still open and Kalus was speeding towards it! Sage exited hibernation mode. 'Reach for the key. It will come to you,' she croaked. Vert reached towards the stormshock and the key shot into his hand.

'We did it!' Vert cheered. Sage flickered and collapsed. Vert rushed to her aid.

'Each time I go through a stormshock, it weakens me. Erases part of my memory. I have travelled far, perhaps too far. I must hibernate.' She returned to hibernation mode, dropping into Vert's hand.

Back at Vert's garage, Sage had been busy.

'My own secret underground base!' Vert was delighted. 'How did you make all of this?'

'With Sentient-based nano-tech. Creating this was simple compared to creating the multiverse.'

Vert was confused. 'Your people created all the battle zones?'

'Yes, but everything that we have created is under attack. The Vandals and Sark destroyed my home world, each taking one of the twin planets. While the Vandals are a tribal dictatorship led by Kalus, the Sark are cold, calculating and deadly robots led by Zemerik. It is only a matter of time before their war spreads to this planet.'

'Not if I can help it,' Vert told her.

'You are a formidable warrior. But you will need help. I have contacted the rest of your team—'

'Team? No. I work alone.'

'I sense a stormshock coming,' Sage said suddenly.

'I'm on it.' Vert suited up and jumped into the Saber, then sped through an underground platform. He heard Sage's voice as he drove.

'Remember Vert, once you enter the battle zone, you must secure the battle key to earth and lock the portal behind you.'

Vert blasted onto the salt flats towards the swirling stormshock. He flew through the portal into the battle zone. In front of him, another portal opened and three Zurk (Sark soldiers) emerged.

Vert raced after them. He pursued them through the twisting streets and rubble of the ruined city, eventually pulling level with them.

They tried to ram him from each side, but he fell back, deploying the Spinning Wheel Blades with a chainsaw-like device from the hood of the Saber.

The blade cut into one of the Zurk's cars, sending it flying away in flames. Vert rammed the other Zurk with his Spinning Wheel Blades, flipping it over. He rounded a corner and spotted the battle key in the air up ahead. The Saber emitted a beam that grabbed the key and secured it to the bonnet. But several Zurk were blocking the way. Vert reversed and hid behind a rock. An evil-looking robot appeared in front of him. It picked up the head of one of the Zurk Vert had just defeated and stared into its face, replaying the last thing it saw. 'That must be Zemerik,' Vert realised. Another robot lumbered up to Zemerik. 'What are my orders, my lord?'

'Find whatever did this. Neutralise it. And bring me the battle key.'

Vert was worried. 'Maybe Sage was right, a team would have been good right about now...'

Back on the salt flats, three cars met, dropping off three men and a woman before speeding away, leaving them stranded. They looked around in confusion. 'This is not a video game convention...' one man noted.

'I was told there was an off-road race,' said the woman.

'The World Mixed Martial Arts Championship,' another man answered, doing an impressive display of Muay Thai moves.

Suddenly, another car arrived. It didn't even stop as a red-haired man and a large stereo were tossed out of the door.

He got up and dusted himself off.

'I say,' he said, switching on his stereo. 'Do you know where the party is?'

Meanwhile, Zemerik had spotted Vert. 'An organic. It has the key!' he pointed to the Saber.

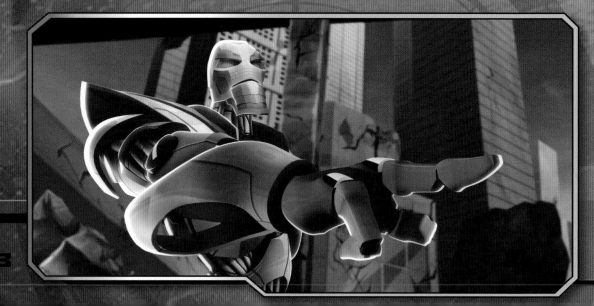

   The Zurk jumped into their vehicles and drove straight at Vert. Vert deployed his wheel blades and shredded two of them. He closed in on another, hitting it head on. The robot hung on to the bonnet of the Saber. 'Zug will smash it,' he growled, raising his metal fist. Vert ejected the windshield, and Zug with it. He drove right through some more Zurk who clung to the Saber. The battle key activated the stormshock and Vert shot through to the other side.

Back on the salt flats, the stranded group were amazed to see a stormshock materialise nearby and the Saber blast out of it. Vert skidded, sending the Zurk flying, and leaped out of the Saber. 'Who wants to help me destroy a pack of killer robots?' he shouted.

The martial arts expert leaped into the air and hit one Zurk in the face with a spinning kick. The other three men leaped into action, attacking the second Zurk. The woman leaped onto the last Zurk's back and ripped its head clean off its shoulders, then drop kicked it into the open portal. Vert reached towards the portal, and the battle key flew out into his hand, sealing it.

On the other side of the portal, Zemerik picked up the Zurk's head. The eye beamed out a holographic image of the scene on the salt flats.

'It appears that I have a new world to conquer,' Zemerik announced.

Back on the salt flats, everybody was staring at Vert. They all began asking questions at once.

Vert held up his hands. 'Chill, guys. Let's head back to my garage, and Sage will fill you all in.'

They had no idea who Sage was, but they followed him anyway.

Back in Vert's garage, Sage explained the mission.

'Why us?' the woman asked.

'Because each of you brings something unique to the team. And you are the best of the best,' Sage replied.

'If we don't work together, our homes and everything we believe in will be destroyed,' Vert added.

'You are civilisation's last and greatest hope,' Sage concluded.

'So, who's in?' Vert asked.

Everybody nodded their agreement.

Back on the Vandals' homeworld, Hatch had made a discovery. 'Captain Kalus!' he called, holding up an ancient-looking television set with an antenna. 'I managed to intercept a Sark transmission emanating from a new world!' Kalus looked at the image. It was the footage of Agura and Vert beheading the Zurk. 'The sub-creature! We shall ravage his home world,' he snarled.

Back in Vert's garage, Sage inserted a yellow chip into the holographic console. 'Zoom, you are nimble and an expert Muay Thai fighter.' The robotic arms moved around him. They pulled back to reveal a new outfit and a bike.

'Awesome wheels!' Zoom cried, checking out a souped-up bike. 'The Chopper!' he decided.

'You will be the team's scout,' Sage continued. 'Agura. You possess great hunting skills. You will be the team's special operations officer.' The robotic arms got to work once more, and pulled back to reveal a new vehicle and outfit for Agura.

'The Tangler,' Agura smiled.

'Sherman, you possess brains and brawn. And Spinner, you possess unparalleled hacking abilities and hand-eye coordination. You both will be the team's strategic tactical and tech support.'

The brothers high-fived and named their new vehicle 'The Buster'.

'Stanford. Your expertise with sound and deadly accuracy makes you the team's artillery expert.' The robotic arms got to work one final time, creating a purple car and a new outfit for Stanford. 'The Reverb!' Stanford smiled.

'And Vert. You display qualities of bravery and fearlessness. You will be the team's leader. You shall be known as…'

'The Battle Force 5,' Vert finished. Spinner looked around and counted the members of the team. 'There are six of us.'

Sherman smiled. 'He's counting vehicles.'

Battle Force 5 were taking a well-earned break in Zeke's diner.

'Let me get this straight,' Spinner said with his mouth full. 'When we're not fighting evil creatures from other dimensions, we pretend to be test drivers for Spectra Motors?'

'That's the cover story,' Vert nodded.

Vert sunk down in his seat as he caught sight of Sheriff Johnson approaching.

'Vert Wheeler,' the Sheriff spat.

'We're not here to cause any trouble,' Vert said. Suddenly the team's wrist communicators beeped. Sage's voice crackled out. 'Stormshock opening in T-minus three minutes.'

'What was that?' the Sheriff snapped. He poked Vert in the chest. 'You better not be up to any funny business, Wheeler,' he threatened. Vert held up a mock salute. 'Yes sir, no funny business. Guys, we've got to jet.' They filed out of the diner.

Back on their homeworld, the Sark were facing the stormshock. 'Prepare to attack!' Zemerik shouted.

On the Vandal homeworld, Kalus addressed the other Vandals. 'Follow me to the portal!' he roared. The Vandals cheered.

Back in Vert's garage, Battle Force 5 were also ready for action.

'Do your best to retrieve the battle key and seal the portal from our enemies,' Sage said.

'Nothing like on the job training,' Vert replied, hitting the accelerator and speeding out of the garage with the rest of the team.

Battle Force 5 zoomed along the flats as the stormshock materialised. 'It's storm-ridin' time!' Vert called as they disappeared into the stormshock for their first mission...